Praise for Storyshares

"One of the brightest innovators and game-changers in the education industry."
— Forbes

"Your success in applying research-validated practices to promote literacy serves as a valuable model for other organizations seeking to create evidence-based literacy programs."   — Library of Congress

"We need powerful social and educational innovation, and Storyshares is breaking new ground. The organization addresses critical problems facing our students and teachers. I am excited about the strategies it brings to the collective work of making sure every student has an equal chance in life."
— Teach For America

"It's the perfect idea. There's really nothing like this. I mean, wow, this will be a wonderful experience for young people."   — Andrea Davis Pinkney,
Executive Director, Scholastic

"Reading for meaning opens opportunities for a lifetime of learning. Providing emerging readers with engaging texts that are designed to offer both challenges and support for each individual will improve their lives for years to come. Storyshares is a wonderful start."
— David Rose, Co-founder of CAST & UDL

Fortunate Fayola

Published by Storyshares, LLC
Inspiring reading with a new kind of book.

The characters and events in this book are fictitious. Any similarity
to real persons, living or dead, is entirely coincidental.

Storyshares
Storyshares, LLC
24 N. Bryn Mawr Avenue #340
Bryn Mawr, Pennsylvania 19010-3304
www.storyshares.org

Interest Level: High School
Grade Level Equivalent: 5.9

ISBN 9798885979023
Book design by Saskia Globig

Storyshares presents

Fortunate Fayola

Stephanie Mhango

Storyshares

1

They say a name defines who you will become in life. Fayola never believed that. Nothing *"fortunate"* had ever occurred to her. Still, she always appreciated the sentiment expressed by her late parents in naming her.

She knew she was not the prettiest of the girls. She was often told that her dark skin and her too-big eyes made people feel like they were being watched by a snake.

Her survival depended on how well she could marry and she was not the most cunning of women. She did not end up marrying well. Her *lobola* (bride price) cattle died of mysterious causes in the first week of her marriage.

She married a farmer who was not good at farming — or fathering. She gave birth to their beautiful son. The farmer ignored him.

The farmer ended up dying at the frontlines, fighting off an ambush raid from a neighboring tribe. Many other men died in that fight as well. The working force decreased, which caused a horrible famine in the village.

Her husband did not have a brother who could marry her, so she had to fend for her son herself. It felt like an impossible task.

2

One day, while Fayola attended to the needs of the king's consort, her problems seemed to be answered. According to the local women, people had begun to take their children into the woods to leave them at the base of an ancient Baobab tree. After three days, these mothers would then return to the tree and find their children plump, healthy, and unharmed, waiting for them. After that, the children would never know hunger, despite the famine.

Fayola and the other villagers had always believed that their tribe had settled on land that was rich with magic. And Fayola was desperate. Desperation can blur the lines between logic and insanity, even for those who don't believe in magic.

So, with the golden heart of a mother but the naivete of a fool, Fayola left her baby bundled at the base of the Baobab. After three days, she eagerly raced to the river to find her child as plump as he was before the famine.

However, he was not there. And so she waited and waited and waited for her son to be magicked to the place she'd left him. But he never came.

3

Overcome with grief and shame, Fayola tore her clothes
and ran to the forest. There, she wandered for what felt like
years. At last, she came to a shabby-looking mud hut in
the deep of the woods.

She knocked on the termite-infested door, hoping that
whoever lived there could spare her some food and shelter
for the night.

An old, wrinkly hag with short, sparse hair answered the
door. Her gravelly voice was the eeriest Fayola had ever
heard. She sounded like five people were talking at once
when she spoke.

Her eyes were small pebbles embedded deep within the wrinkles of her face.

Fayola explained her situation to the old woman. To her surprise, she was met with empathy. The old woman allowed her to shelter there until the morning.

In the hut there were two beds: one made of nails, and the other made of soft-looking heather. When asked where she wanted to sleep, Fayola chose the bed of nails.

When the morning came, Fayola swept the hut and made porridge for the *Ambuya* as thanks. (Ambuya means grand-mother. In many African cultures, younger people do not address their elders by their names, but by the title they would have if they were a relative.)

At breakfast, Fayola was asked if she wanted the porridge bowl mixed with pounded groundnuts and honey, or the plain bowl of porridge without groundnuts and honey. Fayola chose the plain bowl to eat.

As she was about to leave, the Ambuya asked Fayola if she wanted to earn some stale bread by plaiting her hair, or if she would rather relax before continuing her journey. Fayola chose to plait the Ambuya's hair.

4

Satisfied with the character of the young woman, the Ambuya set out to help Fayola. She revealed to Fayola that she was a powerful witch, and told Fayola to follow the path on the other side of the hut.

If Fayola managed to not laugh at the oddities of the forest, or look them in the eye, then she would find whatever it was she was looking for at the end of the path.

The Ambuya gave Fayola a bright red material to wrap around her body to help protect her against the forest's charms. She warned Fayola that if she were to laugh or attract the spirits' attention, she would be snatched by whatever spirit she was laughing at.

Fayola did as she was told. When she could no longer fight her curiosity, she peeked at the spirits with her head mostly covered in the bright red material. Some spirits were as large as trees and some were as small as pebbles. All of them were odd to her. Some glowed, and some were so dark that they looked like they were made of shadows.

As if sensing her curiosity, they began to descend on her. Two spirits started peeling themselves apart in front of her, like their skins were banana peels. It was only the threat of the Ambuya's warning that kept Fayola from laughing at them.

A few moments later, she heard a choir of laughing hyenas that sounded like they had drunk too much *chibwantu* (traditional African alcohol). She ran so that she could not laugh or be heard to be laughing.

She had to out-maneuver and outrun many terrifying beings. She refused to let them seize her or stop her from finding what she searched for.

5

When at last she reached the end of the path, she came to a small shrine. Her heart rose as if threatening to leave through her mouth.

Sitting there, covered in a material similar to hers, was her son. He was plump and smiling at her as if he had been waiting forever for her to pick him up.

Her journey back to the village was peaceful. Even with the laughing and taunting spirits, she felt worthy of her name for the very first time in her life.

She was *fortunate*.

6

Upon her return to the village, Fayola was flocked by many women asking what magic she had used on her son so they could use it on their children too. When she told them about the Ambuya and what happened in the forest, they quickly brought their children to the base of the Baobab tree. Then they put on their most tattered rags and set off for the witch's place.

They entered the witch's house without knocking and demanded that she find their missing children. So she asked them the same questions that she had asked Fayola.

Each time they picked the options easier and most convenient to them. They judged the state of her hut and called her crazy for suggesting that they should sleep on a bed of nails.

By the time the morning came, they were sent onto the path to the shrine without instructions or protective material.

They laughed at everything they found to be odd in the forest. They were even foolish enough to make a deal with an *Ililomba* for gold (an Ililomba is a snake usually made by a witch doctor that is said to grant people magical favors).

Only a few of the women made it to the shrine. And for all their troubles, they found the shrine empty. The women were driven mad with loss.

7

Meanwhile, in the village, the tribe's chief called Fayola to his home. He promised her great power if she could convince the witch to save their village from the famine. He even offered her a marriage to his only son.

She agreed to ask the Ambuya if she would help her village, but only because it would end all the unnecessary suffering. She prepared a basket of offerings for the Ambuya and headed back into the forest.

On the way to the hut, she encountered a hyena that smelt the oxtail stem and lamb meat in her basket. It attempted to charm the basket from her with cunning words, and when that did not work, it threatened to kill her and eat her child.

Fayola wasn't sure whether or not her red cloth would protect her from the hyena's wrath. She clutched the basket to
her chest and ran as fast as she could.

The greedy hyena still longed for a taste of the lamb meat.
He knew that Fayola was off to see the forest witch. He
also knew that the witch, frail in her old age, would likely
be asleep after completing her morning tasks at her ances-
tors' shrine. She would be weak from the day's work.

The hyena reached the witch's hut and swallowed the poor
elderly hag whole.

8

By the time Fayola reached the hut, the hyena had changed into an old woman that did not *quite* look like the Ambuya.

"Oh, Ambuya! What a thin waist you now have!" Fayola exclaimed.

"Yes child, I have been busy with no one to cook for me," the hyena said in its best old-lady voice.

Fayola inched closer, suspicious that something was wrong. "Ambuya! What long hair you have now!" she said. She had plaited it herself not so long ago, and it was now unplaited and down past the old woman's shoulders.

"Yes, my child. I have been using the wild powder I made from all the herbs I collected near my shrine. But you should never ask a witch about her hair unless you want to end up strung to a tree by that very hair."

The hyena growled, growing impatient by the smell of the lamb.

Fayola decided to buy herself time until the real Ambuya came back. "Ambuya," she continued, "what a big mouth you have!"

"'The mouth of an elder may stink, but out of it comes wisdom. So heed my words and do not disturb me from the feast you've brought me!" The hyena sprung towards Fayola and her basket.

They fought bitterly, the red cloth shielding Fayola from the worst of the hyena's blows. The hyena began to vomit from its efforts, and from its stomach, Ambuya's head could be seen pushing against its belly.

Desperate to save her, Fayola viciously swung a broken clay pot at the hyena while it was retching. It fell to the ground, unconscious. Fayola grabbed one of the clay shards and sliced the hyena's belly open, revealing a shocked Ambuya.

9

As a reward for her bravery, the Ambuya put gold inside a remaining piece of the clay pot and gave it to Fayola. She told her that she had enchanted the pot to always overflow with gold. It would not run out for as long as Fayola lived.

Fayola returned to the village a hero, and was revered as "the keeper of the witch's fortune." Her people would never know hunger again.

About the Author

Stephanie Mhango is a contributing author to the Storyshares library.

About the Publisher

Storyshares is a publisher focused on supporting the millions of teens and adults who struggle with reading by creating a new shelf in the library specifically for them. The ever-growing collection features content that is compelling and culturally relevant for teens and adults, yet still readable at a range of lower reading levels.

Storyshares generates content by engaging deeply with writers, bringing together a community to create this new kind of book. With more intriguing and approachable stories to choose from, the teens and adults who have fallen behind are improving their skills and beginning to discover the joy of reading. For more information, visit storyshares.org.

Easy to read. Hard to put down.